tHE LIttLE bIRD WHo HELD tHE SKY UP WItH HIS FEEt

Paro Anand is a writer, performance storyteller and children's-literature activist. She has headed the National Centre for Children's Literature at the National Book Trust, India, and runs 'Literature in Action': a programme designed to encourage creativity amongst young people.

In 2006, her book, *No Guns at my Son's Funeral,* was included on the International Board on Books for Young People (IBBY) Honor List as the best book for young people. *The Little Bird That Held Up the Sky with His Feet* is on 1001 Books to Read Before You Grow Up—a list of the world's best books of all time.

Ajanta Guhathakurta studied Fine Arts at the College of Art, Delhi, and has worked as Art Director at Penguin Books India. She is now a freelance illustrator. In 2002, Ajanta received the Certificate of Honor presented by the International Board on Books for Young People. She can be contacted at ajantastar@gmail.com.

tHE LIttLE BIRD WHO HELD tHE SKY UP WItH HIS FEEt

A MODERN FABLE

PARO ANAND

Illustrated by
AJANTA GUHATHAKURTA

RED TURTLE
RUPA

To my parents
Pran and Sarojine Chopra
And
Kuldip and Harshi Anand
For holding up my skies,
Always

. . . .

Published in Red Turtle by
Rupa Publications India Pvt. Ltd. 2013
7/16, Ansari Road, Daryaganj
New Delhi 110002

Sales Centres:

Allahabad Bengaluru Chennai
Hyderabad Jaipur Kathmandu
Kolkata Mumbai

First published by HarperCollins Publishers India 1993

ISBN: 978-81-291-2117-2

10 9 8 7 6 5 4 3 2 1

The moral right of the author has been asserted.

Typeset in Adobe Garamond Pro 15/19

Printed at Repro Knowledgecast Limited, Thane

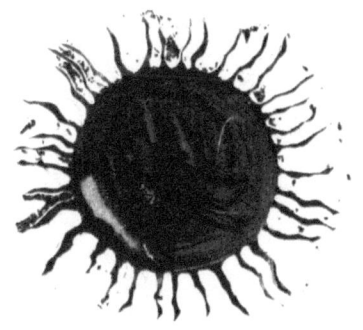

ACKNOWLEDGEMENTS

To Julia Eccleshare and her team at 1001 Books to Read Before You Grow Up for giving my little bird new wings.

To Mona and Nona for their laughter.

To Aditi for letting me get a glimpse into her world and to Little Red Car Films with my blessings.

To Uday whose Human Dimensions will give wings to so many families.

And to my Keshav, without whom I would not, could not fly.

But most of all to Berna didi for giving us all such a comfortable nest to come home to.

Thank you all for all you do for me.

BOOK ONE

FEARS, PLANS AND NEW HOPES

The forest stood still. Anxious. Waiting in fear and dread as the past rolled into the present—a present that was as bleak and dismal as the grey clouds that were banking low over the forest canopy.

The animals that gathered in groups below the still, solemn trees spoke in whispers, as though to keep their fear a secret from the eavesdropping clouds above.

The whispering and trembling of the animals made them resemble the leaves of the trees under which they had taken shelter.

But the shelter was temporary and soon the raging storms would catch everything that moved. They would hunt out the fox from its lair, the lion from its den. They would wash away the nest of the starling and flush out the smallest creature which sought cover underground. Even the fish who lived in the water suffered when the inevitable flood came. The fish whose life was water were dashed against rocks and suffocated because of the silt which thickened their very life source. The flood caught them all. Every one of them. It had done so before. It would do so again.

'And there's nothing we can do about it,' pronounced Crow—ever the voice of doom. 'Absolutely nothing!'

'You mean we can only wait?' yelped Dhole, the wild dog.

'Wait and watch?' echoed Jackal, staring with jealous eyes at the brave, fearless Dhole, whom he both hated and admired.

'Wait and watch and DIE!' gloated Crow who took pleasure in others' misfortunes and feasted off every death.

'Oh!' exclaimed little Mouse Deer as tears escaped her big, soft eyes.

'Hush, hush now,' soothed Hare, trying to console Mouse Deer. They had both lost their children in the previous year's flood. And they had young ones again this year. They could not be sure that their little ones would survive this fresh threat.

Just then, Elephant came swaying by. She too had her young one following behind her.

'Oh Elephant,' called Hare, 'have you any news to give us about what's happening in the forest?'

'Any hope to offer?'

'Has anyone thought of a way to save themselves?'

'Or us?'

Elephant came lumbering up to the knot of querying animals. Anxiety showed on her great face. A few more wrinkles folded into her wide forehead and the restless swaying and probing of her trunk indicated to the waiting animals that the news she had could not be good.

'Ah, what hope? What news can I give to you, my little brethren?' she sighed and snuffed up a little dust, making Mouse Deer sneeze. 'Though it breaks my heart to go, I must...'

'Go?'

'Go where?'

'Sneezz'

Elephant continued, 'Though it breaks my heart to go, I have decided to leave this godforsaken forest. It has been my home since my birth and I have reared many young here. But of late, I am losing more children and family members than my old heart can bear and so I have taken the terrible decision to forever leave this forest where the sun will not shine.'

Her knowing eyes were moist and her trunk sought out her calf for comfort.

'But, but Elephant!' exclaimed Mouse Deer, wide-eyed with wonder, her mind hardly able to take in such enormous thoughts and plans. 'Where would you go?'

'And how do you know you'd be safer there?'

'The way would be full of many dangers unknown...'

'I know,' sighed the great matriarch. 'I know well that dangers unknown lurk along the path that I seek to tread. But surely it is better to risk possible obstacles than wait for a flood to carry my calf away, which I fear is a certainty.' She hesitated a moment, fanning her doubts with her great ears. But then she shook her mighty head as she came to her decision and, nudging

her calf with her trunk, she said, 'Come my young one, we must flee now before the clouds trap us in their arms of dread and death.

'Farewell my little friends, young and old, and may you live to see better times when the sun smiles down more kindly upon this sodden forest.'

With that, she lumbered away, her young calf trotting trustingly behind her.

The animals were sorry to see her go. She had been a good and dependable ally to them. They well knew that their jungle would never be the same without her.

'But she's right, you know,' sighed Dhole, 'the floods are coming for sure and our homes will be washed away...Perhaps we too should follow the path she treads.'

'NO!' shrieked Jackal in fright. 'How, how can you, or Elephant, or for that matter anyone be sure that the floods will come again this year?'

'Yes,' whispered Hare softly, as if scared to express hope. 'After all, a few years ago, it would only rain enough for the lakes and rivers to fill, for the forest to be refreshed, and then the sun would shine again. Perhaps, this year too...?'

'Right, how do we know for sure that the rain will come, that the sky will fall upon us and wash our homes away?'

Birds of all shapes and sizes—Starling, Egret, Parrot—had been gathering all this while in the trees above the arguing animals. Even the tiny, insignificant sparrows stilled their fluttering to listen. At last, Parrot spoke, 'The rains, I fear, WILL come. And come in destructive sheets. It is inevitable.'

'But why?' persisted Jackal. 'How can you say this with so much certainty?'

And Parrot explained to all those gathered there that it was not a question of chance any more. The mountains, up to which their forest stretched, had once been

green and lush with deodar, chir and pine trees. But now they were stripped naked. Brown and bare. They held no water to their hearts. So when the monsoon wind and rain swept down their slopey sides, there were no trees to break the force before the monsoon hit the forest. The earth, no longer held together by tree roots and grasses, was stripped bare. Rivers would choke and thus the floods would come.

'...and so, you see, I fear the worst. The

monsoon clouds gather overhead and mock our fears and feeble plans. The floods will come. They must.'

The group was silent, thinking, wondering. Then timidly, the Mouse Deer spoke, 'Wh-what if we said some prayers? Surely someone, somewhere would listen. This forest's gods must hear us?'

'Huh! This forest has no gods.' That was Crow again, speaking in sarcastic tones as always. 'Don't you remember that the peacocks danced and prayed for seven nights and days last year, and still the floods came?'

'Yes,' agreed Dhole. 'And the monkeys. Remember they offered sacrifices and performed great penance the year before, hanging upside down for hours on end.'

Crow looked smug while the group fell silent once again.

Suddenly, the brooding silence was rent by the mighty roar of King Lion. A few moments later, his messenger fleet, the

eagles, came shrieking shrilly from above.

'The king summons all his subjects—high and low—to a most important meeting...'

The hills around echoed their cry:

Meeting
　　　...eeting
　　　　　...ting
　　　　　...ing
　　　　　　...ing...

The eagles swept past, slicing through the rain-heavy clouds, repeating their message for all to hear. The animals stopped to listen and watch until the birds were out of sight and only the echoing hillsides reverberated with their presence.

The animals looked at each other; there was hope in their eyes, although none dared to voice it. Perhaps the meeting had been called because their king had found a way to save them.

'A meeting?'

'What about?'

'Of what use is a meeting when our lives are threatened?'

'But go we must if the king has summoned us...perhaps he has a plan?'

'Plan or not, we must go.'

'For who dares disobeys King Lion?'

And so, all the animals of the forest, from the swiftest gazelle to the slowest snail, gathered around the great crag of rock that served as King Lion's throne. As he mounted the top-most rock, the animals bowed in respect. He had been their king for many years now, and there was no lion old enough or strong enough to challenge his supremacy. He wore his battle scars like medals to prove his undisputed strength. A deep scar slashed over from the corner of his left eye, across the bridge of his nose and disappeared below his golden muzzle. The older animals remembered the fearsome battle their king had fought with a young male who had wandered in from a neighbouring territory. The fight had almost killed the older one as the two lions battled late into the night. The animals, shivering in their dens had heard terrible howls of pain and growls of fury. No one could tell who would be vanquished and who would be their king at the end of this Great Battle.

In the morning, there were signs of battle, but none at all of either lion. It was only three days later that their old king emerged, weakened from blood loss and injury, but still supreme and still their reigning king. What became of his challenger, no one knew, but stories abounded that their king had killed and eaten him. No one knew for sure. The stories soon became animal lore. Certainly, after that, there had been no other challenge, either from outside, or from within the jungle itself.

As the animals gathered, they found the king flanked on either side by his ministers who sat on lower rocks according to their ranks—the great Eagle, the lustrous Butterfly, the restless Monkey, the cunning Fox, the night-prowling sleek Black Panther and the silvery Masheer Fish. They looked a grand gathering, but obvious worry lined every face as it turned to King Lion who cleared his throat and began to speak.

'Friends,' he began in his rich, heavy voice, 'we are not gathered here for any light or frivolous purpose as, I am sure, you are well aware. I can well realize your anxiety and concern over the approaching monsoon. I know how troubled you all are by the memories of the havoc caused by the floods of previous years.'

A buzz of agreement went up from the crowd. They well knew what he was talking about.

'It has come to our knowledge that this year's monsoon is posing an even greater threat to our forest than ever before.'

Fear thickened the air around the gathering and every animal held its breath.

'But, I will let your minister give you the information first hand, for the eagles have been to survey the situation...'

He turned to Eagle who alighted on a higher rock and addressed them, wings outstretched. He was always an impressive sight, but today, his voice was grave.

'Friends, as our king has already suggested, I too must admit that the news is not good. My kin and I have flown over every part of our jungle and its surrounding neighbourhood. The hillsides lie brown and bare and the river banks are cut away and damaged by previous floods. The rain clouds overhead are filled with rain and will burst forth without delay. There seems no way to prevent the flood which once more threatens our homes and lives. I... we...you...' The Eagle Minister's wings drooped in defeat. He no longer looked

the Prince of the Skies as his voice choked with emotion and he stepped down, unable to speak further.

A short silence followed before the king himself could speak. 'Now,' he continued, 'I have called this meeting not to offer any solutions, because, frankly, I have none...'

A discontented murmur rippled through the gathering and rose to fill the air. The lion was disconcerted, if not surprised. He silenced his subjects with a sharp snarl, 'I know that you will be disappointed. I know you have come here full of hope of finding a readymade solution. But the problem at hand is neither so simple nor so easily solved singlehandedly. I have honestly tried to find a way, as have each of your ministers to come up with some sort of solution. But...'

The murmur rose again as the dreaded word 'but' sank like a stone on their fragile hopes.

'But...' continued King Lion, trying to ignore the growing restless discontent in his ranks, 'but we have no shame or remorse in admitting that no solution has presented itself to us, despite our best efforts.' The crowd grew sullenly silent.

'I know a simple, permanent solution to our problem would be so ideal, but in the absence of one, I have an offer to make, for I too feel the same tension and anxiety as you do. So, listen carefully now, to my offer.' The crowd leaned forward. Perhaps there was a way, after all. They held on to their king's every word as he continued.

'Whoever can think of a solution to this problem will be made my second-in-command, senior to all my ministers. He or she will sit on the highest rock to my right. Now, I give you all three days to think over, discuss and work out a solution, cover all possibilities. I know that three days seem too short a time, but that, the eagles

tell me, is about all the time that we have left before the sky falls upon our heads. We will meet again on the third day to see if anything suitable has come up. I don't think that I need to urge you all, for ours is a common cause. Three days, then. And until then, I take leave of you with my best wishes. Thank you!'

With that, he rose majestically and swept out of the meeting. He made his exit with as much confidence as he could muster—a confidence that he did not quite feel. This was the first time in all his many years as king that his absolute authority had been put to such a test. He could not but help question himself about his right to the throne. For if he could not ensure the safety of his subjects, what right had he, or his chosen minister of the skies, land and rivers to hold on to their positions? A low, troubled rumble escaped him as he thought, 'If some animal really does come up with a solution which has escaped me thus far, why should he only be my second-in-command? Why should he not be the king himself?'

He shuddered at the thought of being ruled by a lesser animal—Porcupine, Hare or worse, the slavish Jackal. And yet, how wonderful if one amongst these or any other creature could actually find a way out. Was it possible? Was there a solution somewhere, lurking in the heart of some unknown creature? Hope and dismay waxed and waned within the breast of the anxious king as he made his way back to his lair.

In the meantime, the animals of the forest gathered in groups to discuss what their king had just said. For once the groups cut across every distinction. Deer mingled fearlessly with Dhole, and Peacock with Panther. The fear of the threatening rain clouds made each one forget its mortal

enemy since they were bound by one common concern.

Most of them were bitterly disappointed and could barely hide their disgust at the king's inability to solve this most critical problem in years. They had hoped for some flicker of an answer, and finding none only deepened their despair.

'Huh!' complained Porcupine, all bristly with anguish. 'If the king and all his ministers put together can't offer a solution, what do they expect *us* lowly commoners to do?'

'Quite right!' whistled Lapwing, looking sleek and efficient as she prepared to fly off to her nest. 'What's the king there for if not to solve our problems?'

'Ah, but...' reasoned Hare, 'don't you think you're being a bit harsh? After all, the king admitted failure despite his best efforts.'

'Best efforts, shest efforts BAH!!! We

29

didn't see a single one of these so-called best efforts, did we?'

'But be reasonable,' answered Hare, getting rather tired of Crow's gloom, 'even the king is only an animal, not a God. He never claimed to be more powerful than the Monsoon Army.'

At the very mention of the name Monsoon Army, an involuntary shudder shot through the assembled animals. Mouse Deer crept into the sheltering shadow of Panther.

'I don't think that we should be wasting our time in picking faults with our leaders,' growled Leopard. 'They've told us to find a solution, so let's focus on that. Yes, let's go and catch those who are responsible for our misfortune and deal with them.' His snarl was fearsome and some wary animals slunk away into the gathering gloom, sensing a change in the predator's mood.

'Who do you think Leopard meant when

he said we should catch those responsible for our misfortunes?'

'Could it be the Monsoon Army?'

'No, you fool, he meant Man who is the reason the hillsides are stripped of their protective cover of trees.'

'Battle Man? But how would we even begin to do that?'

'We have no time to do battle with Man, our adversary, though it is none other than he who we have to blame for denuding our forest. It would be an impossible battle anyhow. They have weapons that can far outstrip any of ours. Now when our trouble looms large over our heads, it is better for us to put our hearts and minds to saving our forest home.' Hare spoke in a voice of calm reason that stilled the restless crowd. They saw now that it was by far the only sensible thing to do. However impossible the task ahead seemed to them, it was only fair that each one put his mind to finding

a way. Who knew, perhaps there was one.

'Ah well,' sighed Slow Loris sadly, 'how wonderful it would be if *I* could think of something wise and wonderful to solve this tangle and become strong and powerful. But...' she shook her little head, 'I don't suppose I'll ever be so clever.'

The animals dispersed now, for dusk was falling. Every bush, every blade of grass stirred as animals, insects and birds bedded down for the night. Those for whom the day

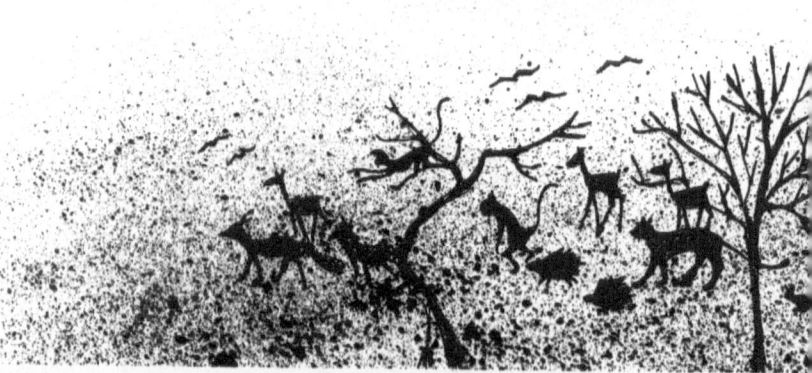

had just begun—the nocturnals—well, they were already awake and were soon striking out to fulfill their natural needs. But each one's mind was troubled by one thought, and not on the business of sleep or hunger. Some dreamt of death and destruction while others had pleasanter dreams of becoming heroes overnight.

The night was unusually quiet, for the crickets too were deep in troubled thought. Who knew what tomorrow had in store?

The monkeys decided that the answer lay with them. They thought of building a giant umbrella that would shelter them from the onslaught of the monsoon. They gathered large leaves and requested the tailor birds to sew each leaf together. They all got busy. The trees willingly gave up their biggest leaves and the tailor birds worked ceaselessly, morning to noon, noon to night, stopping only when hunger and exhaustion got the better of them. At last, a huge sheet of matted leaves was ready. Monkeys and birds got together to lift the contraption to the tops of the tallest trees. Screams, shouts and shrieks rent the air as instructions flew faster than the birds, back and forth, back and forth.

Higher
Lower
Faster
Slower

The huge green sheet was lifted inch by painful inch. It seemed as though it might very well work.

Yes
   No
      Stop!
       Go!
        OH!!!!
         NOOOOOOOO

The sheet sagged at the centre, under its own weight. Creatures big and tiny struggled to lift it to the tops of the trees. The leaves at the centre began to separate. Quick as lightning, the tailors were back, rapidly repairing the tearing seams. But then, there was another. Then another. In the flurry of the tiny darting tailor birds it was hard to tell one bird from the other. But try as they might, the leaves continued to separate and give way, until, with one loud

OHHHHHHHHH

of disappointment, the sheet gave way and collapsed on to the cheering fearing animals below.

The monkeys and tailor birds were stunned and totally disheartened as they sat still and exhausted, disappointed beyond tears. There was total silence all around.

The second day, the burrowers got together—hare, weasels, moles and snakes.

'We'll dig a huge pit,' suggested Hare. 'We'll slope the sides down. Then all the water will flow in and make a lake...'

'That's a great idea, that way we'll be saved from the floods and have water for the dry season!'

They tried it. They did their best. But all they really managed to achieve at the end of the second day was to expose roots and in many cases, cut the roots of some of the forest's good sturdy trees. This angered the wiser animals.

'You have weakened trees; they may not

withstand the vagaries of the coming winds and water.'

'And what about our homes?' grumbled the tree dwellers. 'Once these trees too collapse, what will become of us? Where will we go?'

The monkeys were especially querulous. More so because their own plans had failed so miserably. They jeered and heckled the burrowers who alternately squabbled amongst themselves and mocked the monkeys' own failure.

The forest heaved with restless discontent as fights broke out. Bystanders joined in and took sides supporting friends against foe, or even foe against friend. The threat that loomed large literally above their heads only served to make each inhabitant more edgy and bad-tempered than ever before.

And so, the days passed. As the third day dawned, animals prepared to make their way to the meeting place. Anxiety had transformed to frenzy and now was quickly descending the slippery slope into panic and then despondency. There had been so many plans that failed. So many squabbles, so many hopes and dreams dashed. But there was no plan that held out a single ray of hope, at least, no one had heard of any such.

The animals began gathering from early dawn. Today, the assembly of animals was quiet and a pall of gloom hung over the heavy-hearted beasts and birds. Silence lay thick as, heavy as the moisture-laden clouds that hovered above. A mild, retreating sun smiled weakly and sadly as Lion mounted King Rock and began proceedings.

'So friends, we meet again. Now, I would like all animals, birds, water-dwellers, er... insects, whoever has suggestions to come forward one by one to present their ideas

to us all. Let us hear out the plan, after which we will have a discussion on its feasibility and, if necessary, we can actually put the plan to the test. Do you all agree?'

The animals nodded doubtfully. They were not convinced about the need for discussions and experiments. And most didn't understand the big words he used. But who could question King Lion? Besides, perhaps, just maybe, there was such a plan. So they nodded in agreement.

King Lion proceeded, 'Very well, now, all creatures with plans and ideas, step forward and make a queue, we will hear your plans one at a time.'

The king and all his ministers looked around eagerly as did the forest folk. But all was quiet and still. Not one creature broke ranks to step forward.

'Come, come,' rumbled Lion, as a growl escaped his throat, 'come, come surely someone has a thought or idea…?'

Yet, the stillness was like a spell cast over the uneasy gathering. The animals watched as their king's face began to turn a particularly angry shade of gold. Yet, not even a leaf stirred to break the fearful spell of doom. No one had hoped for much, but surely something, anything would be better than this. This sham.

And then, just when it seemed that the jungle was doomed to disaster, just when it seemed that all was lost, there was a little flutter from the back. Eagerly, the animals turned their heads, but immediately any hopes raised were dashed to the ground, as who should come tremblingly forward, but Piddi, the tiny little sparrow—the lowest and commonest of all the birds!

The animals parted to let him pass through. They sniggered as Piddi went past. He looked a pathetic sight, shaking with fear and awe from ashy-grey head to dust-brown claw.

A stifled ripple of laughter accompanied him, growing and spreading like a wave as he shuffled his way to the top of the group. The laughter grew and grew until all the animals were caught in the throes of their mirth at the very ridiculous thought that a common sparrow had the audacity to consider himself the saviour of the forest, and worse, for the commander-in-chief's post. The laughter did them some good too, as it pulled them out of the quicksand of gloom into which they had sunk. Even King Lion had a smile on his royal face when he saw that it was only a sparrow that emerged from the throng of subjects.

As Piddi reached the head of the gathering, he stopped as though too afraid to break contact with the comfort of the crowd, the security of being just one fragment of the whole; the comfort of tiny, dusty anonymity. But the Eagle Minister caught his eye and urged the little bird to step out and come forward.

Piddi was finally out in the open, he looked even smaller now that he stood apart from the mighty herd. In fact, he practically faded, merging into the dusty earth he stood on.

King Lion spoke with a smile on his face. If nothing else, this would divert the anxious crowd for a few moments. 'Yes, yes, come forward, little one…' But hearing his mighty voice so close, Piddi fluttered

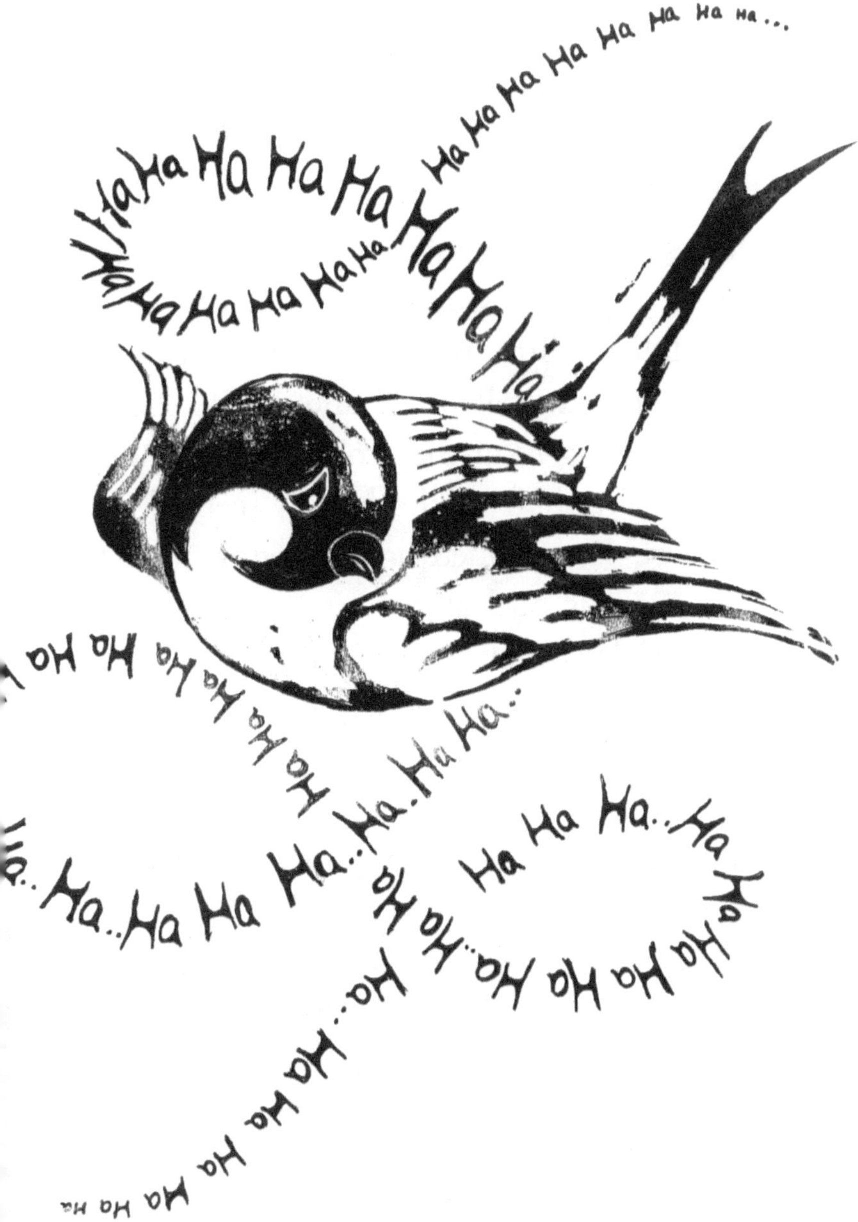
Ha Ha Ha Ha Ha Ha ha ha...

his wings, making to fly away. 'Come now, don't be afraid, we want to hear what you have to say.'

Piddi inched up, sidling up on to the lowest of the rocks, trembling so hard it seemed that he would fall right off!

'Tell us, little bird, what are you called and then, do tell us all about your...er... plans?' King Lion tried to smile his kindest smile, although to the bird it seemed like a snarl. He nodded again, trying to help the nervous bird along.

'S-s-sir,' began Piddi, 'Oh m-mi-mighty sir and a-all g-ga-gathered here. I-I am P-P-Piddi, the sp-sparrow,' he started, but immediately stopped as the sniggering transformed itself into laughter that engulfed the crowd.

'Quiet!' commanded the king and everyone fell into an immediate sulky silence. 'Yes, Piddi, tell us your plan.'

'Your m-majesty, I know that I'm v-v-v-

very sm-small,' the little bird started again, 'b-but I think I've a p-p-plan that may just work, s-s-sir.'

'Yes, yes, let's hear it,' encouraged Eagle, secretly proud that one of his fellow birds had come forward when all others stood back silent, blank. Even the crowd listened attentively, although more out of curiosity than hope.

'Sir,' continued Piddi, feeling a little braver now, although he still cast his eyes down to the ground and spoke into his feathery chest. 'Your majesty, sir, you see, it's like this, well, it's not a plan really, but since our last meeting I have been having a most peculiar, most *real*-er-d-d-dream!'

'Dear God, we're trying to find a way of preventing floods and he's telling us all about his er—um—*dreams!!*' spat Crow disdainfully.

Other animals too were beginning to turn away, lose interest. But to Piddi, it made not a shred of difference. He didn't hear or see or even notice the restless wave that rippled through the crowd. He continued.

'And in this dream, your majesty, I'm just sitting in my tree and the sun is shining nice and bright...' Piddi smiled a little at the sweet, distant memory of his dream.

'...and so, we all lived happily ever after!' mocked Crow crudely mimicking the smaller bird.

'Or maybe he'll wake up to find that it's raining,' laughed Hyena, collapsing into a fit of giggles.

'Hush, ssh! Keep quiet, can't you?' admonished Hare. 'Either come up with a suggestion of your own, or hear him out.'

'Yes, give him a chance,' hissed others.

But to Piddi, none of the interruptions mattered. He was now deep in the world of his dream. His voice had changed, become deeper, slower and his eyes were glazed and strangely focused as he spoke on.

'And in this dream, I'm sitting on my tree and the sun is shining very brightly. But soon, I notice that it's getting hotter and hotter and brighter and brighter. This goes on until...until, your majesty, sir, my eyes are completely dazzled by a great shining light which is awfully close to me on my tree! It is scorching hot as I shield my eyes and squint to try and see what's happening. And yes, it is the very Sun himself, sitting right next to me, on my own tree, on MY OWN BRANCH!' Piddi's voice rose into a squeak.

A loud, disbelieving snigger broke from the crowd, but was quickly hushed by a sharp look from Eagle. In any case, not one creature made any move to leave the meeting now. Each one was secretly eager and was filled with hope against hope that there was more than just a little bird's imaginings in the story that unfolded before them.

'Of course,' continued the tiny bird, still unaware of his surroundings, 'I'm terribly frightened and awfully hot, but anyway, I ask, "E-excuse me sir, but—but are you the SUN?'

'"Oh yes," answers Sun softly and surprisingly close to my ear,' said Piddi, his beady eyes growing wider and brighter with excitement.

'"Little bird," says Sun to me,' continued Piddi, his voice no longer a reedy chirrup, but taking on, instead, a deep, golden tone when he spoke for the sun.

'"Little bird, I know how all the animals and forest dwellers are worried at the approach of the Monsoon Army..."

'"Oh yes," I reply and he continues, "You know little bird, I'm worried too, because if it rains too much and the floods destroy your jungle, it isn't just bad news for you, it's bad news for me too."

'"Why, Mr Sun?"

"'Because, wee one, it means that I would have lost my battle with the Monsoon Army again this year. And, well I can't very well go on losing year after year, can I?"

"'Oh no, sir," I agree, "you can't, but—but I don't understand, why are you telling me all this?"

"'Ah, I'm coming to that," says Sun, sadly shaking his mighty golden head. "You see, Piddi, it just so happens that you, little bird, you are the only one who can help me win this year."

"'ME? Me? Oh no, Mr Mighty Sun, there must be some mistake. Surely you should go to Parrot, he's so clever, or Peacock, he's so handsome, or Eagle who is our Minister for Bird Affairs. Or…or you could go to the tigers who are so fierce and fearless, or Deer, even, for his swiftness, or—or—or oh, ANYBODY. Any, anybody, dear Sun, would be more appropriate than me. I'm the tiniest, plainest, and most insignificant of all the creatures. Why, even Butterfly, who is smaller than me can change herself from a hairy caterpillar into the most gorgeous…NO! NO! There's been some terrible mistake; I'm s-s-sorry…"

'I'm, I'm crying now, in my dream,' explained Piddi to the king and his ministers, 'I'm crying, panicking, but…'

'But?' asked Parrot, urging him on.

"'There is no mistake, Piddi," says Sun, talking softly and calmly in the face of my hysterical outburst. "I don't want to go to

Parrot or Tiger or Peacock; if they could help me, I would have gone to them instead. However, as it is, little bird, I have come to you because you are the only one who can help me and help your jungle. Now listen carefully to what you must do—listen well, for there isn't very much time left…"

The gathering of animals leaned forward to hear the tiny bird's soft brave voice unfold the mighty Sun's plan.

"'It's like this, you see,' says Sun to me, "first the Monsoon Army comes, as it is supposed to. The first rains are good for us. We all know that. We know that no rain is bad, perhaps even worse than too much rain. However, the Monsoon Army never knows when to stop and it starts raining more and more and too much more. More than any forest would ever need. That's where I come in and start *my* battle. I'm supposed to break up the army and chase it away. This is something that I have been able to do, over seasons and centuries. But now, now the Monsoon Army, over the years, has gathered great strength and is being led by a new, ruthless commander and is more intent on fun and destruction than doing his Rightful Duty. I am no longer able to break them up as easily as I did. I can no longer chase them away when their work is done.

'"Now, year after year, they stay on to plunder and destroy. This year, little bird, it has come to my knowledge that the Monsoon Army has terrible things in store. Terrible plans for your jungle..."

'Terrible things? Terrible plans?' the forest gathering echoed fearfully as the bird spoke on.

'"...this year, Piddi, the Monsoon Army has sworn to tear apart this jungle of yours. It has sworn to destroy every living creature. Every tree or plant that dares to bloom and grow."

"'But—but why, Your Majesty Sun? Why *our* jungle?"

"'Yes, I'm coming to that, little one. You see, the Monsoon Army has showered great destruction on this jungle, year after year. And yet, as if to mock its most devastating efforts, your forest rebuilds itself anew. Plants spring up forgetful of the rainy months and animal young frolic in spring-fresh grass. You prosper despite the Monsoon Army's hatred and they cannot stand that. They feel threatened by every flower that turns to fruit and every flock of birds that takes wing."

"'And so they've threatened to destroy us, oh Sun? Every last one of us?"

"'Everyone, little bird, every last one of you. Forever!"

"'Forever?!"

"'They will tear apart and shred everything that crosses their path. They will rip the very sky open in their viciousness, little bird;

they will rip open the sky and cause the heavens to collapse on to earth in a final, mighty destructive deluge…"

"'But—but, oh Great Sun, all of what you say must be true, but what's any of it to do with me? I don't even have an egg of my own, nor a mate.'"

"'It has everything to do with you, Piddi, for it is the very fact that you have no personal investment. For the actions you take will be for Greater Good. And only for Greater Good. It is your very humbleness and insignificance, your complete lack of grandeur which makes you stronger than any beast. Stronger than me and, I hope, mightier than the mighty force of the Monsoon Army. If anybody is invincible, it is you, little Sparrow!'"

"'But sir, I don't see…I mean me? Invincible? How?'"

"'Are you willing to try, Piddi?'"

"'Sure, sir, but, but try what?'"

"'Are you willing to try to save the forest?"

"'Save the forest? Why of course, of course I am. I'd do anything I can to save the forest."

"'You'll have to do more than just what you THINK you can. You will have to go beyond the strength and willpower you feel you have. You will have to go deep down within yourself and look for and find things you never knew were within you. For you, tiny one, have abilities and qualities that you never realized you had. You are capable of more than your meager little form suggests."

"'I can? I mean, I have? Can you tell me how?"

"'Yes, now listen Piddi, listen with all your attention."

A hush had fallen on the forest gathering. The leaves on the trees had come under the spell of the tiny bird's brave words. It seemed that the world had stopped on

its axis and was standing still in awe and admiration of little Piddi bird. He spoke slowly but firmly, deep in the web of his reverie. He spoke on. And every ear strained to hear his words.

"'Little Piddi, yours is an all-important role, and now I will tell you how you must play it. When the rain first starts, you must lie out in the open, flat on your back, with your feet in the air. You must keep your feet steady and strong for they must support the weight of the entire sky. When the Monsoon Army arrives, it will see how insignificant, ordinary and tiny you are. They will rain on, at first soft and slow, then harder. But you will not relax. Not for a single moment. Steadily you will hold the sky up with your feet. The monsoon will be irritated, upset by your audacity. It will start making efforts to tear at the sky, at the forest, and the forest dwellers. And most of all, little bird, the monsoon will try to tear at you. But you must be strong in your body and your heart and your mind. You must shut your eyes and keep them tightly closed for the faces of the army clouds are mean and frightful. The mere sight could well make you weak with fright, for just a moment. And one single moment is all they need to rip up the sky. Then all will be lost. So hold the sky up little Piddi, hold the sky up with your feet, for all of us!"

'And with that...' concluded the sparrow, coming out of his reverie and addressing the assembly, 'with that, my dream ends, but, as I awake, I feel a strength inside me, in my legs especially, but...' He smiled bashfully as his voice trailed away and he looked around at the faces of the animals and birds gathered around him. Not one of them was sneering or sniggering anymore. They were all staring at him intently, almost in awe! He looked so different now from the

dusty, trembling bird that had stepped on to the high rocks but a few moments ago. He held his head high and his eyes were bright with a new confidence. His chest feathers were puffed and were being ruffled by a breeze which made him appear larger. Stronger. Indomitable.

King Lion was the first to speak, his voice somber with thought, 'Well Piddi, and what do you intend to do now?'

Piddi stood still a long moment, thinking, considering. Then he spoke. This time, his voice was brave and strong and his words were clear and sparkling like a mountain stream that knows its path well.

'Your Majesty, honoured ministers and friends of the air, land and water. I believe that there is some truth in all that I have dreamt these last two nights. If you all have faith in me, I will do my best to follow the sun's instruction and hold the sky up with my feet. Small and insignificant as I am, I

think—I believe—I believe that I can do it!'

A wild cheer broke out from the crowd. King, ministers, birds, beasts, fish and insects alike joined together to cheer their stout-hearted little warrior. To those towards the back, he looked like a mere brown speck against the rocks and beasts that ranged and towered around him. But he was no less significant for he stood rock-steady with confidence radiating from him like the sun's own warm rays. Not one of the creatures assembled there thought of him as a mere sparrow now. He had been transformed into Piddi the Saviour who was justly being accorded a rousing applause.

Indeed, so loud and thunderous was the cheering that it was a few moments before anyone realized that the Enemy had arrived. The dreaded Monsoon Army was already issuing its first battle cry with a threatening roll of thunder and an ominous flash of lightning in a frightful show of strength.

The cheering soon melted away, as smiles gave way to worried frowns. The dreaded moment had arrived and now they could only hope and pray that what Piddi had spoken of had had some truth and was not just a fantastic dream of glory.

As the first, fat, warm raindrops fell, the animals scattered, running helter-skelter for shelter. In the space of a few chaotic moments, little Piddi found himself quite, quite alone in the middle of the deep, darkening forest.

BOOK tWO

tHE BAttLE

Piddi the Sparrow looked up to face the mean, black clouds as they rent the air with another vicious clap of thunder, slapping the sky with the full force of their fury. For a fleeting moment, his legs buckled underneath him and his courage drained away at the thought of the daunting task that lay ahead of him. At that moment, he didn't feel so strong and brave. He felt like the dusty, ordinary common sparrow that he had always thought himself to be. He wasn't ready to be the hero of the jungle; wasn't ready to take on a battle that the mighty Sun himself could not win. Grave, dark thoughts flooded his mind and weakened his spirit. He wanted to just fly to his tree and shelter there. Hide his head under his wing. And if his branch was torn away, if his tree blown down, so be it. What could he, a little sparrow do about it? He had never wanted fame or power. Let those with family and young defend the forest and fight the Monsoon Army for their sake. Why should he, who had not yet a mate or allegiance to a nest, die for a forest full of animals who had never even acknowledged his existence? And even if he did put up his bravest and best fight, surely the terrible army would shred his efforts within minutes. He was no match for them and he was no martyr.

'Let Sun choose someone else, not me. Never me!' swore Sparrow to himself as

he was assailed by wave after wave of self-doubt. Flooding him much like the rain was preparing to do.

Once again, he cast a dubious eye heavenwards to face his adversary. Piddi saw the sun look down on him and give him a look of such desperate anxiety that it touched Piddi's tiny, fluttering heart. He wanted to cry out to the sun, to appeal to him to choose another soldier to fight his battle, to let him off from this terrible task. But the sun was driven back, back and further back by the darkening clouds until he was out of sight and Piddi's plea was left unanswered.

The army uttered a low, threatening growl that rumbled and echoed through the forest, sending every animal trembling deeper into its lair.

Piddi turned his wee head homeward and spread his brown-grey wings to fly back to warm shelter when a needle-sharp drop was sent like a stinging arrow into his scrawny shoulders. It was a challenge, a gauntlet flung down by his foe. He heard the clouds above laugh a sneery laugh. They laughed knowing they had already won the battle before it had even begun; that the sun himself had fled the battlefield ahead of the rampaging army. That there was no obstacle now in their path of destruction.

Quick. Quicker than the lightning that lit up the flashing sky, Piddi turned once again. This time more resolutely, away from the comfort of the familiar branch that had served as his home for so long. Piddi flung himself down on to the ground and turned himself over until he lay flat on his back, his tiny breast bared to the onslaught of the quickening monsoon rain. He braced his legs and he closed his eyes and he shut out all the doubts that had so weakened his resolve a moment before. The little bird's forehead wrinkled in anxious concentration

as he gathered all his strength into his feet. He braced his legs, flexed his claws. He quickly glanced at the cloud's face leering low over him. An unknown battle had begun for Piddi the little sparrow against the formidable Monsoon Army.

At first the clouds did not even notice him lying there on the ground. The rain-splashed earth so merged with his speckled feathers that there was nothing to notice. The clouds, in fact, were so sure that they were unchallenged this year, that they did not care to look around for resistance. This time they were relaxed, in no hurry to get on with their job.

The rain began slowly. Kind drops spattering into the thirsty earth. Then the pace quickened and the drops came down more sharply. The little bird sensed the change, felt it on his bony body. He was soon soaked to the skin and his breast caught the brunt of the sharp raindrops that

stung him mercilessly. The wetness soaked through the soft, downy feathers on his chest, making them stick to his body and reveal the frightened fluttering of his beating heart. The rain ran down his beak and into his eyes, making them sting and smart. But Piddi remembered all the sun had said, and kept his eyes tightly closed. And his feet steadily held up the turbulent, heaving sky.

Soon the rain was coming down in sheets and it wasn't long before every rivulet was gurgling and swift, every waterhole brimful of sparkling water to sustain the jungle through the hot, dry months of summer. The trees were washed, their leaves sparkling like diamond-encrusted emeralds. The forest was rejuvenated for the rain had been good and had done its job. And, no doubt, done it well.

Now it should have been the sun's turn. Now the black clouds should have rolled away to give way to clear blue skies and the sun's life-giving warmth to nurture sprouting saplings and ripening fruit. Now, it should have been the monsoon's end.

But that, of course, was not to be. As every animal strained to hear the welcome sounds of distant thunder calling the rain-bearing clouds away to other hills, they heard, instead, the coarse voices of the army as they clashed and crashed and revealed their monstrous plan—just as the sun and eagles had predicted.

'Ah! Our work is done...' they rumbled in their thundery, wet voices.

'...now for some play!'

'Yes, let's destroy this sodden jungle once and for all!'

'For all time to come, let this jungle stand as a testament to our indestructible strength and invincibility!'

Yes! Yes!
Let's shred the sky!

Let's tear the sky!
Let's destroy the sky overhead!
And make it fall…
with a crash…
with a flash and a crash…
Let the sky fall on this forest…
this puny miserable forest!!!
This jungle that has dared to bloom
in the face of our destruction!
Ha! Ha! Ha!!!!
Our fun has just begun!

The animals heard the clouds and whimpered in hopeless fright. Surely one little sparrow could not match the might of this terrible enemy. Parents nuzzled their young and could not help but wonder if it was for the last time.

Piddi heard the army too and every threatening word. He lifted his beak skywards and flexed his feet which did not, for a single moment, falter. The battle had only just begun in earnest.

The clouds tossed and turned the sky. They pulled it this way and that. Their task was surely an easy one and victory would be assured and sweet. But what was this? The vengeful clouds, so blinded by their pride and wrath, had not yet noticed the little bird whose minute feet held the sky up in staunch support. Now they were taken aback. The sky that they had expected would come apart and fall away like autumn leaves in the breeze, instead held out, and held fast.

'Hey? What's this?'

'What's happening here?'

'Is there someone who dares to challenge us?'

Like clumsy giants, they rushed about from one corner of the jungle to the other. They were searching for some great beast whose might challenged theirs. But there was no Sun, no Elephant, no ferocious predator

to be seen. With satisfaction, the monsoon clouds sent probing fingers of icy winds and saw that every living creature cringed into its lair to escape detection. The trees bowed their crowns in humble submission. The clouds rushed about scenting victory on the wind and they carelessly spent their force all over the jungle.

They set about their task again, tearing at the sky. But again, it would not submit. Who was holding on so strongly to the sky? Between searching and tearing and snapping at the sky and each other, the clouds quite overlooked the little wet, brown bird that lay on the wet, brown earth. The clouds grew more wrathful and irritated and their efforts grew more ferocious and tempestuous, more intimidating.

But Piddi was not intimidated. He held the sky up with his feet.

Then a cloud, hovering low, heavy with rainy destruction spotted the wet, dripping

bird. Its contemptuous mirth knew no bounds as it unleashed its fury on the little bird almost driving him into the slushy ground on which he lay, almost burying him in mud and water, gleefully preparing a slushy grave for him

'Look!' the cloud boomed. 'Look at this half-dead insect that has the nerve to think that he can put up a fight against nature's most powerful army!'

The others crowded around to see. Their shrieking laughter rent the air and every animal trembled in his lair and wept with despair and anguish. This was surely the end. What the cloud said was true. Piddi was too small to defend them.

But Piddi did not flinch. He did not wince, not even when all the clouds, together and in full strength unleashed their icy loads on to his fragile breast. He did not flinch when the accompanying wind ruffled his wet feathers with deathly cold fingers.

'Ha!' the clouds responded to his efforts. 'Look, just look at him, this shivering lump of feather and bone does not even dare to look us in the face...'

'And yet he thinks that he can hold the sky up?'

'With his pathetic little feet and legs that are no thicker than a single raindrop?'

'Does he really hope to control *us*—the All-Powerful Army?'

'Does he really hope to keep us from having our way?'

'Oh bird! It is us who are the Lords of the Sky, not the sun.'

'He has already admitted defeat, you know that don't you?'

'After all, there is only one of him and so many of us.'

'And, little bird, there is barely even one of you...you can hardly hope to hold us off, let alone defeat us...'

'Give up, little bird, give up while there

is still life in your body.'

But the bird held on.

'Oh ho! You frighten me, oh Strong One, with your fearsome muscle-bound body!' mimicked and mocked a cloud and the others responded by shrieking with laughter. When they failed to budge him, the clouds grew impatient and more bullying.

'Go away, insolent creature, and let us get on with our play!'

'Get up, go now, before we have to kill you.'

'Get up!'

'GET OUT!'

'GO!!!!!'

They whipped up a frenzied tempest and tore at him. The wind wrapped its long icy fingers around his little legs and tried to force them down.

Piddi heard their scornful voices and he felt every tug as he was buffeted and tossed. But he did not, would not weaken.

'Open your eyes, little bird,' wheedled a voice next to his head, a soft, seductive voice. 'If you have so much strength, have the courage to look your enemy in the eye...' But the bird kept his eyes squeezed tight. He would not look.

And yet, it rained and it rained within the forest and the little bird was beginning

to tire. He was now weak from cold and hunger. His body and spirit trembled at the thought that his test was, as yet, a long one and he was already being overtaken by exhaustion.

Not one animal had dared to come out of its hiding place to give the sparrow any sustenance or support. Now they listened and watched fearfully, peering out into the rain-lashed jungle as they prayed fervently that Piddi would be their saviour.

The brave little bird never once opened his eyes. He knew that the evil faces of the monstrous clouds would frighten him and weaken his resolve and his frail feet. He knew, for the sun had told him. He knew that he had to be infinitely strong and make no mistake. So he kept his eyes tightly shut and thought of all that the sun had said to him.

'You'll have to do more than just what you THINK you can do. You will have to go beyond the strength and willpower you feel you have. You will have to go deep down within yourself and look for and find things you never knew were in you. For you, wee one, have abilities and qualities that you never realized. You are capable of more than your meager, tiny form suggests...'

Piddi recalled the sun's warm words in his dream. He recalled them and hung on to them like a drowning animal hangs on to shreds of floating wood. He warmed himself with those words and strengthened his legs with them. Now more than ever before, Piddi really wanted to DO something. Do it well and succeed. He

knew that what the sun had said was true, for Piddi searched deep within himself, searching and finding the will to hold out. He seemed to be hovering somewhere between reality and dream. Sometimes he felt the sun's great heat on him and sometimes the lashing rain's icy presence. He was no longer sure which one was real and which his imaginings. One thing he could feel for sure. One thing he knew was real. The entire enormous weight of the vast sky rested upon his tiny feet as it was tossed, turned and torn by the enemy army.

'NO!' he thought fiercely to himself, 'No, I will not give up. Never. I'll do this. I will win this. I will. I MUST!'

And how the army fought. They teased and tossed and turned and tore at the sky.

'HO! Little bird,' they sneered, 'have you had enough, or you still want to play with us some more?'

Again the whispery voice lingered near his ear, telling him about the warm safety of his nest, luring him with kind words to loosen his grip on the sky.

But the little bird held on. And on.

The army flashed in fury, turning to strategy now. They took turns. While some rested, others fought a pitched battle against the bird. They hoped, of course, that somewhere, somehow, Piddi would weaken and give way. That would be their chance and they would need no other. They would tear up the sky, making it fall on the heads of every forest creature who lurked there. But no, Piddi would not weaken.

He held on.

He was beyond cold now, beyond hunger, beyond even exhaustion. His legs were so stiff with the exertion of having kept them upright, that, perhaps, they would not bend, even if he had weakened. He felt no awe now and he felt no fear. He just held

84

the sky up with his feet.

'Little bird...' burbled a watery voice right next to him, so close that it seemed to be coming from his own head, '...little bird, we'll make a deal shall we, hmmmmm?'

The bird didn't turn his head or give any answer, but the voice, slimy like stagnant, stinking water went on, 'You go back to your tree and we'll leave you alone. Always. We'll destroy everything else around, but we'll leave you. Quite a deal, don't you think? Wouldn't that be wonderful though? Just think. You wouldn't be a nobody anymore. Why, you'd be the King of the Jungle. Lord of all you survey.'

Another voice joined in, 'Oh wouldn't that be nice. You in your nice, warm cosy nest. So put your legs down bird, just, just for a moment, really. Oh nobody would ever get to know you gave in. I promise you that. Nobody would know that you had made a deal with the enemy. Just

one single moment, relax
your grip now and let us tear
at the sky. Remember, you could
be king, little bird. Quite safe, quite
warm. Instead of dead!'

Not a single muscle of the bird flickered
in acknowledgement of the wheedling
voice's bribe. Not a twitch or murmur.

'...well, be quick, quick now, puny one.
For we haven't got time to wait about. We
must be off to other lands. So, have you
decided, what is it to be?

'A deal or—or DEATH?'

But Piddi would make no deal. He
would not rest and he held the sky up,
untiringly, with his feet.

'FOOL!' shrieked the voice, no longer
the whiny wheedle, but one that was cold
and hard and furious as the rain turned into
hail. 'FOOL! You have lost your chance.
We have no more patience with insolence
such as yours. You have thrown your life

away uselessly. Now we will prevail.'

The animals watched in dread and awe as the clouds tore. They tore at the little bird's fragile body, rent the turbulent sky and whipped up such a storm that it became difficult to see through its fury.

But Piddi held on with his feet and the sky would not tear.

At last, it was the Monsoon Army that tired. It was the Monsoon Army that spent its mighty force uselessly. In vain. It was the Monsoon Army that turned white with shame and slowly rolled away to let the sun come shining through. It was the Monsoon Army that lost the battle against little Piddi the Sparrow!

BOOK tHREE

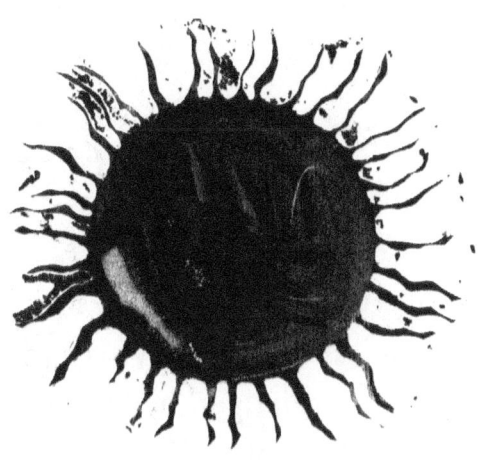

...AND tHEN...

The raging storm gave way to sweet silence.

A smiling sun emerged in cobalt skies and sent down his soft, golden mellow warmth. Slowly, trees lifted their bowed heads and swayed hush-hush in the soft breeze. A blackbird's trilling rolled through the crisp, clear air, its notes carrying true and sparkling. Streams renewed with fresh, unmuddied water, gurgled with happiness. This year, they were not filled with angry, roaring waters. Silvery fish splashed glinting, and dragonflies rippled the now still, calm waters.

Cautiously at first, the forest folk stepped out of their homes. They could hardly believe that the danger had passed. They looked in wonder at their forest, as if for the first time. This year, the jungle was not ravaged and plundered. This year, it was washed and green and revived. And, wonder of wonders, the sun shone gladly down upon the happy scene. A rainbow lit up the brightening sky.

Piddi the Sparrow, commonest of all creatures had actually saved them and their forest home.

Piddi was now to become the king's second-in-command. His Chief Minister!

King Lion came out, followed by his ministers. Other animals jostled each other as they approached the clearing where their hero still lay on his back, feet tightly

clenched, up in the air.

Sun's rays slanted in salute as they fell in gratitude on the little bird as King Lion cleared his throat to address him in a voice full of admiration.

'Arise, Piddi, arise, my brave warrior, Saviour of the Forest. Arise and receive your prize. For this is your hour of glory!'

But Piddi didn't stir, and his eyes did not open. He just lay there, still supporting the now calm sky with his feet.

'Piddi,' Parrot gently nudged him, but the sparrow was cold and still and stiff all over. 'Piddi…?'

Piddi was dead.

The effort of holding the sky up had been too much for one so small. But he had held it up. Held it up with all his

might. And more. Much, much more. He had won his last battle. Piddi was no longer the lowly sparrow that few even noticed. He was Piddi the Hero. He had, as the sun had said he would, found strength and will within himself far beyond the strength he thought he had. He was common, he was frail, he was ordinary. But he had saved the forest. He had saved them all. And no one would ever forget the great battle he had fought. And no one would ever forget what the little bird had done for them.

EPILOGUE

And ever since that day, whenever a bird dies, it dies flat on its back, with its feet held stiffly up in the air, in honour of Piddi, the little bird who held the sky up with his feet...